How Many Spots Does a Leopard Have?

AN AFRICAN FOLKTALE

Retold by M. J. York • Illustrated by Elizabeth Zunon

The Child's World®
1980 Lookout Drive • Mankato, MN 56003-1705
800-599-READ • www.childsworld.com

Acknowledgments
The Child's World®: Mary Berendes, Publishing Director
The Design Lab: Kathleen Petelinsek, Design
Red Line Editorial: Editorial direction

ISBN 9781614732174
LCCN 2012932870

Printed in the United States of America
Mankato, MN
July 2012
PA02123

nce upon a time, a leopard lived in Africa. Leopard was very vain. His coat was covered in beautiful black spots. He spent as much time as possible admiring them. He would hold up his paws to watch the sun shine on his fur. He would spend hours gazing into a still pool looking at the spots on his face and back.

One day, Leopard was lying on the lakeshore, gazing at his reflection and dipping his tail in and out of the water. He was singing softly to himself about his beautiful spots.

Plover the shorebird waded over. "Leopard," she whistled, "what are you singing about?"

"I am singing about my spots," replied Leopard. "Aren't they beautiful?"

"They are," answered Plover. "But how many spots do you have?"

Leopard let out a long, thoughtful purr. "I've never counted them," he admitted. In truth, Leopard did not know how to count.

"Could you count them for me, Plover?" asked Leopard. "There are too many spots for me to count them myself."

Plover hid her laughter behind her wing. She knew Leopard could not count. But it would not do for Leopard to see her laughing. After all, he could eat her in one bite. "No, I am sorry," she replied. "I must get back to my nest." And she waded away, still laughing softly to herself.

Leopard was frustrated. Now that he had the idea to count his spots, he wanted immediately to know how many spots he had. He left the lakeshore and went in search of someone who could count his spots.

Soon, Leopard found Tortoise sunning himself on a rock. "Can you count my spots?" Leopard asked.

Tortoise considered this for a moment. "Yes, I believe I can try," he replied. Then, he cleared his throat and began.

"One!" he called, pointing to a spot with his first leg. "Two!" came next as he pointed to a second spot with his second leg. Then "Three!" and "Four!" with his third and fourth legs. Finally, he counted "Five!" with his tail.

"You have more than five spots!" declared Tortoise.

"Can't you count higher than that?" asked Leopard.

"No," replied Tortoise. "I need my legs and my tail to keep track of the numbers."

"Well, do you know what comes after five?" asked Leopard.

"No," said Tortoise. "Why don't you gather all the animals together? Surely someone can count your spots."

So Leopard sent invitations to all the animals. He offered a magnificent prize to the animal who could count his spots. The next day, all the animals met beside the lake.

Monkey had the first turn to count Leopard's spots. She counted ten spots—

"One, two, three, four, five, six, seven, eight, nine, ten!" Then she started over again—"One, two, three, four—"

"Wait!" exclaimed Leopard. "Why did you start over?"

"It's multiplication," answered Monkey. "We can count how many groups of ten there are. Then we multiply and know how many spots you have. Two tens makes twenty. Three tens makes thirty. You see?"

The other animals stared at Monkey and scratched their heads. They did not understand multiplication. After all, most of them could not count!

"Well, if you do not like my method, I'll go count something else!" said Monkey. And she swung off through the trees.

"Can't anyone count my spots?" sighed Leopard.

"I can only count to six," said Mouse. "That's how many children I have."

"I can count really high," said Eagle.

"You can?" asked Leopard eagerly.

"Yes," replied Eagle. "I can count from high in the air! But I can only count to twelve. Thirteen, eighteen, sixteen—so confusing."

"Oh," said Leopard glumly. He was becoming sure that no one could count his spots.

Giraffe spoke up. "Your spots are almost as beautiful as mine," he said. "I counted to fifty once. I can count your spots!"

So Giraffe began to count. "One, two—oh, my, that is a lovely spot. Three, four, five, six—that one is shaped like one of my spots. Seven, eight—but is that one spot or two?"

The other animals came closer to take a look. They began to argue loudly. Leopard couldn't hear himself think. "Quiet, everyone!" he yelled at last. "These are my spots, and I say that is two spots."

Everyone agreed that was fair, so Giraffe continued counting. "Seven, eight—"

"Stop!" called Leopard. "You counted seven and eight twice."

"Oh, dear me," said Giraffe. "Usually I can count very well. But your spots are so beautiful it's distracting."

Giraffe tried again. He counted the spots on Leopard's tail—thirty-seven. He counted the spots on Leopard's head— twenty-two. But no one knew how to add thirty-seven and twenty-two. Leopard also suspected that Giraffe counted the most beautiful spots more than once.

Giraffe started to count the spots on Leopard's body. But when he got to sixty-nine, he paused.

"Does anyone know what comes after sixty-nine?" he asked. The animals began to argue again. "Seventy!" said Tortoise.

"No, eighty!" argued Eagle. They argued for several minutes before deciding it was seventy. By then, no one knew which spots Giraffe had counted already.

"This is too tiring!" sighed Giraffe. "I'm going to take a beauty nap. You'll have to count the rest without me."

Since no one could count as high as Giraffe, the animals started to leave the gathering. Then Jackal raised his head. He had been watching everything from the edge of the group.

"This counting is all wrong," he said. He walked in a circle around Leopard, looking at the spots from all angles. "It is as I thought!" explained Jackal. "Leopard has only two spots. He has dark spots—" and Jackal touched a dark spot with his nose. Then, Jackal touched a place between dark spots where Leopard's fur was light. "—and he has light spots!"

"Oh, clever Jackal!" cried the other animals. "Leopard has light spots and dark spots!" One by one, the animals left the lake. Soon, Leopard was left looking at his reflection by himself.

Leopard didn't think Jackal was right. But since he could not count, he didn't have a better answer. So Leopard gave Jackal the magnificent prize—a picture of himself!

FOLKTALES

How Many Spots Does a Leopard Have? is a funny, and frustrating, story. Did it make you laugh when all the animals could not count? Or were you frustrated with their failure? A story like this one is called a folktale because it has been told for many years, passed from one teller to the next. Folktales often include fantasy elements, like animals that can talk, to keep our imagination alive. Such stories also inspire us to learn or try something new, in this case: counting.

This folktale originated in Africa, a large continent with many climates, habitats, and animals. We can count fourteen different animals in this folktale. Can you go back through the pages and find them all? You may recognize some of them from the outdoors around you, and others, like the lion, may not live where you do.

The bear counts the highest, making it to twenty-nine leopard spots. How high can you go? Try counting the leopard's spots on each page of this book to find out.

ABOUT THE ILLUSTRATOR

Elizabeth Zunon grew up in a hot, sunny country in Africa called the Ivory Coast. She loved to draw, create dances, and play dress-up when she was a little girl. As she grew up, she didn't change! Elizabeth now lives in upstate New York, where she stays warm by dancing around the living room— paintbrush in hand.